The Saggy Baggy Elephant

A Golden Book ● New York
Western Publishing Company, Inc., Racine, Wisconsin 53404

Sooki was a happy and carefree little
elephant who lived alone in the jungle.

Every day, he danced cheerfully
by himself: one-two-three kick,
one-two-three kick.

Then one day, a saucy parrot laughed at Sooki's saggy, baggy skin.

This made Sooki very sad. "What can I do about all these wrinkles?" he asked.

"Try exercise," said a beautiful, sleek tiger.

But exercise didn't help a bit.

"Try soaking in water," said the parrot. "Maybe your skin will shrink!"

But a great big crocodile snapped at Sooki and chased him from the water.

"I'll hide in a dark place where my bags and sags and creases and wrinkles won't show," Sooki told himself sadly, and he slipped into a cave.

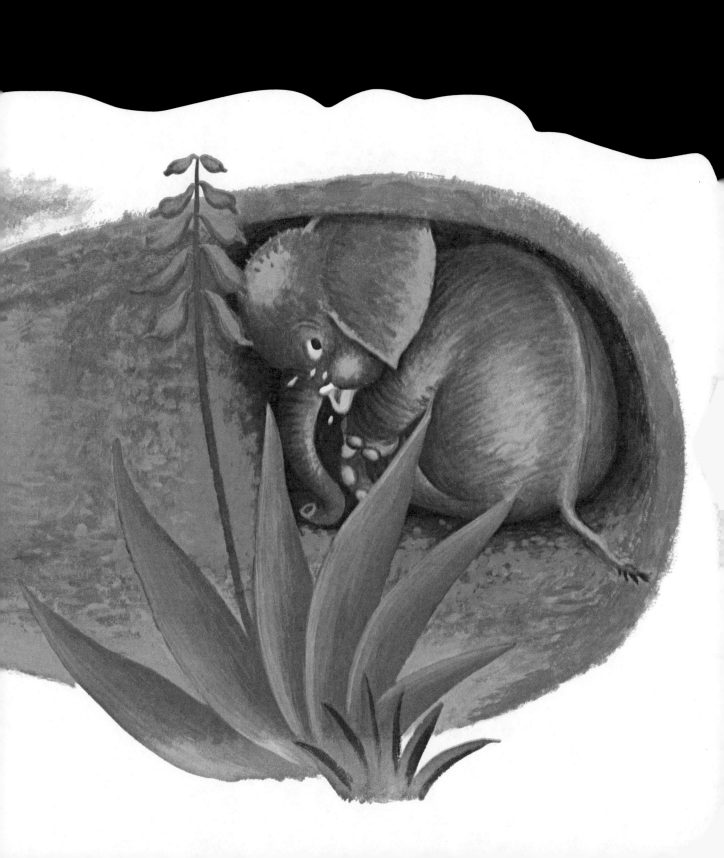

Suddenly the loud roar of a hungry lion shook the jungle.

"I'm so hungry I could eat an ELEPHANT!"
cried the lion, and he headed right for the cave.

Sooki was so frightened he couldn't move.
He let out one great trumpeting bellow.

To his surprise, a whole herd of huge, gray, *wrinkled* elephants appeared and frightened the lion away.

They gathered around Sooki and smiled at him. "What a beautiful little elephant!" they all agreed.

Sooki was so happy that he began to
dance, one-two-three kick, one-two-three
kick, through the jungle.

And all those big, friendly, wrinkled
elephants danced behind him.